Out of the Blue

Copyright: Colette Makray

Published: March 2013

Tess pulled herself up out of the lake from her early morning swim and walked carefully over the smooth pebbles of the shoreline. She loved how they massaged her feet, the perfect ending to her morning workout. She lifted her goggles on top of her swim cap and grabbed her towel from the dock. The lake was cool this time of year, the early summer sun had not yet warmed its gentle waves and there was a crisp breeze in the air. Tess quickly wrapped the towel around her shoulders and shivered like a child fresh out of the bathtub.

She loved this place, the sandy beach, the stacked granite steps and the towering pines that surrounded the Lodge. She even loved the pine-planked boat dock that reached out into the lake; the very place where her husband had died almost two years ago. Tess found it so ironic that a 38-year old man who loved adventure and had risked his life many times for the sake of a good thrill, died while he was fishing, peacefully at the edge of a tranquil lake. Certainly not what his high school friends would have expected when they wrote "don't die doing something stupid" in his yearbook. But in a way, dying the way he did was exactly the kind of thing Tom would do, something completely unexpected. The thought made Tess smile as she glanced up at the Lodge. Beckett Lodge was stunning this time of morning with the pumpkin orange sun reflecting off the windows like fire. Everything was peaceful, for now.

Later, the Lodge would be a buzz with activity when Tess welcomed two new guests and their dogs for a one week stay. Tom had always taken care of check-in, but with him gone, it was her responsibility, just like everything else; cleaning the two guest cabins and main Lodge, maintaining the grounds, keeping the boats afloat, preparing the food, and catering to her visitors' every need.

Tess whisked away the thought, vowing to enjoy her last few minutes of solitude alone on the beach. She spread her beach towel over the uneven sand, sat down and stretched her thin tanned legs out in front of her. She folded at the waist to get a closer look at a dark brown spot on her thigh.   As she studied it, Tess heard the faint sound of splashing coming from the lake. She lifted her hand to shield her eyes from the sun and peered out from the beach. The sun made the lake sparkle and dance and the reflection was almost blinding. She squinted and scanned the water.

Then she saw something. She could just barely see the outline of an object toward the center of the lake. She blinked hard to focus and stood to get a better view. It was definitely moving closer to her, swimming not drifting, bobbing up and down and making the occasional splash. It was too big to be a duck or a loon yet it didn't swim like a person. "What is that?" Tess questioned. Her pulse quickened slightly as she inched closer to the edge of the shoreline. It looked like an animal. Tess moved out knee deep in the water. Then the figure came close enough for Tess to see what it was. "It's a dog!" Tess shouted. Her Speedo goggles snapped from the top of her swim cap as she dove back into the lake, racing toward the animal.

"Okay, boy, I think we're ready. Let's get the rest of this stuff loaded up." Brandon reached down and gave the dog, whose head was firmly nuzzled next to his hip, a scratch before slinging the last remaining bag over his shoulder. He grabbed his truck keys from the small wooden table beside the door and reached for the latch just as his cell phone rang. He paused and considered not answering it, he knew who was calling. It was his boss, Police Lieutenant James H. York.

"Hello" he answered.

"Bishop? You better be on your way out the door!" The voice on the other end was stern and serious.

"Hey Lieutenant, yep, we were just leaving." He shifted his weight to one leg and rolled his eyes.

"Well son, enjoy your week off and hopefully once you get back here, you'll be in a better state of mind."

"Thank you, sir."

"If there are any new developments in the Porchman case, I will give you a call and let you know."

Brandon Bishop hung up the phone and muttered a few words under his breath. James York had been like a father to him since he started on the force 10 years ago and Brandon knew his heart was in the right place, but the constant support from his boss was making him feel like a charity case. They both knew that one week at a vacation Lodge with his beloved German Shepherd and K-9 partner wouldn't help him forget what happened. But his boss was adamant, insisting that it might help him get his head back in the game.

He readjusted the pack on his shoulder, swung the key ring around his index finger and signaled for Toto to come. The confident but aging Shepherd limped to his side. Brandon gave him a quick rub under his chin and the two walked out the door.

Brandon lifted Toto into the truck; his hips wouldn't allow him to jump like they used to. Brandon hated that Toto was getting old. For the past nine years they had been more than just partners, they were roommates, teammates and best friends. Brandon wasn't ready to lose him, not yet. Brandon especially despised the rumors floating around the department that Toto was getting too old to do his job. They had made a mistake, screwed up, it was that simple and it had nothing to do with Toto's age or lack of ability.

But, like clockwork, Brandon's rational thoughts were strangled away by guilt. If he and Toto hadn't spent so much time wrongly searching the neighbors shed, they would have gotten to the little girl in time. She was only a few hundred feet away.

Brandon grabbed the wheel and pulled himself into the truck. He scratched his head and tried to regroup. They had a long drive ahead of them and the whole point of the trip was to try and come to terms with what had happened and move on. Toto whined and inched closer to him.

I'm sorry Boss. I know the mistakes we made are causing you a lot of grief. I wish things had gone differently and we were able to save that little girl, but there was a reason I spent so long searching that shed. It wasn't wrong for us to be there, you'll see. I always have your back and you know I would do anything for you.

"Okay, Toto, what CD do you want to listen to?" He tried, like he had for the past six months, to focus on something else. Toto started to pant and looked eagerly out the front window.

"Pearl Jam it is", Brandon announced and slid the CD into the disk drive. He cranked up the volume to try and drown out his thoughts. As he backed out of the driveway, he hoped that a solid week of swimming, fishing, and relaxing with Toto would be just what he needed to shrug this whole thing off.

"Mommy, when are we going to be there?" the five-year old asked from the backseat of the car.

"We still have a long way to go Gavin," his mother responded.

"I want to get out. Can we find a park and stop to play?"

"Oh Gavin, I'd rather just keep driving, we'll get there faster that way." She hoped the child would accept her dismissive explanation.

"But driving is so boring. I want to stop and play for a little while!"

Joanne Lawrence would do just about anything to avoid one of her son's epic meltdowns on this road trip, even if it meant letting him have his way. She certainly wouldn't be able to handle one of his ferocious temper tantrums right now, not with everything else she had on her mind. If a few minutes of play time would avoid an hour of screaming, then that's what she was going to do.

"I think there's a little park coming up," she told him.

"Mommy, can Derby play at the park too?"

With even the slightest mention of the dog's name, Joanne could feel her temperature start to rise. She clenched her teeth and paused knowing that Gavin would not take no for an answer. She loathed her soon-to-be ex-husband for surprising their son with a puppy last Christmas, a puppy that had turned into a massive 120-pound beast that she had to feed, clean up after and pretend to like. He did it just to spite her – what else was new - and she was sure he was taking great pleasure in her misery. Even this trip was ruined because of his careless decision. Instead of staying at a 5-star resort, she and her son were forced to choose a pet-friendly Lodge because there was no way Gavin was going to leave that stupid dog behind.

"Mommy! Can he?" The child yelled.

"We'll have to see how busy the park is Gavin. If there are lots of kids playing, there may not be room for Derby, okay?"

"If Derby can't play at the park then I'm not going to either" Gavin pouted.

Joanne peeked in the rear-view mirror and watched as her son wrapped his scrawny arms around the dog's neck and buried his face in his colossal mane. They were such a mismatched pair, her boy was small for his age, almost impish, and the dog was enormous, one of the biggest Saint Bernard's her vet had ever seen. Of course, her husband picked the biggest dog he could find and Joanne was sure he did it just to make her life as difficult as possible.

As they pulled into the rest station, Joanne could see there was a little park off to the side and right now there were no other kids. Perfect. Now the boy and the dog could get out and she could have a few minutes to herself. She really needed to call her agent and touch base; she was dying to know whether he had heard back about her audition. And she wanted to go over the divorce papers one more time before she signed them and sent them back.

She watched as the boy and the dog made their way to the park. She found it odd that somehow Derby knew not to pull too hard at the end of his leash and risk dragging the little boy to the ground. Joanne was thankful that the giant dog seemed to have a keen sense of his size and strength and never overpowered her son. At least there was one redeeming quality about him. She shook her head and slid her cell phone out of her purse as she watched her son head for the playground.

"C'mon Derby, let's go and play. I'll go down the slide and you watch me at the bottom," the child instructed as he climbed to the top of the ladder.

Okay Gavin. But be careful up there, you'll hurt yourself if you fall. I'll be here at the bottom waiting for you. I know you count on me to be there for you and I will never let you down. I will always be there. You are my very best boy.

Tess's arms darted out in front of her as she stabbed through the lake water with a sense of urgency she hadn't felt since her last high school swim competition. Without hesitation, she was racing out to an animal she knew nothing about, never considering that this dog might not be friendly or rabid for all she knew. But for Tess, it was pure instinct to save a helpless creature.

As she approached the dog, Tess tamed her stroke from a panicked frenzy to a calmer stride. She didn't want to startle him so she spoke softly as she swam up alongside. The dog turned, responding to her voice and began to paddle towards her. He was a good swimmer and now that Tess was close enough, she could see he was a beautiful blonde Golden Retriever. He looked just like Mabel; the Golden that she and Tom had always joked was their honeymoon baby because they adopted her nine months after they were married.

Mabel was their inspiration for opening Beckett Lodge, a place where people could vacation with their dog and never have to worry about their pet's safety and well-being while they were away. Tess and Tom weren't so fortunate with Mabel. She escaped from a kennel while they were in the Caribbean for a friend's wedding. The kennel owner said that Mabel bolted from her enclosure and escaped through an open door before anyone could stop her. Tess and Tom spent every waking minute searching for their lost pet but she was never found. Their heartbreak was unbearable and their anger and frustration fueled their determination to open a vacation property for people and their dogs. Beckett Lodge opened 4 years to the day that Mabel disappeared.

"Hey there buddy" she whispered kindly to the water-logged animal. "What are you doin' out here in the lake all by yourself? I'm just going to swim alongside of you here until we get a little closer to shore and then I'll give you a hand okay? You're probably pretty tired, huh?"

Tess guided the dog toward the beach. Surprisingly, he wasn't struggling or showing any signs of fatigue and as the two swam side by side, Tess wondered how long the dog had been swimming and where he had come from. She decided that once they reached the shore, she would have a clearer head to try and figure it all out. Right now, her priority was getting the dog safely out of the lake.

Tess felt the sandy bottom of the lake on her toes and dug them in to pull herself into shallower water. She stepped toward the dog and cradled him with one hand under his belly and the other under his neck. The dog stopped paddling his legs in relief. Tess's feet sunk into the gritty bottom like quick sand under the weight of the dog. She could feel that he was wearing a collar; the metal dog tag was digging into her arm. Good. Once they made it to the beach, she could see who this dog belonged to.

As the two reached the smooth pebbled shoreline, Tess released the dog and watched as he scrambled to the beach. He stood and panted with exhaustion, shaking his saturated fur from side to side. Tess walked to her beach towel on the sand, still beckoning her to sit and enjoy the morning sunrise and collapsed to her knees. She hadn't swum far; much less then she swam each morning but the sudden rush of adrenaline had left her exhausted too.

The dog bounded to where she was sitting and sat at her side, nudging her arm with his muzzle.

"Well you seem to be in good shape," Tess said as she looked him over for any sign of injury. "And in good spirits," she chuckled as the dog continued to push his cold wet nose into her arm. "Are you trying to say hello or thank you?" She gave her new found friend a scratch under his chin and behind his ears. "Well, hello to you too, and your welcome. Now let's have a look at your tag and see where you're from."

The bone shaped metal tag dangled from the loop of the loose fitting and slightly frayed red

woven collar. As Tess reached for
it and pulled it toward her, the
metal caught the reflection from
the sun and made her squint. The
tag was faded but she figured
when it was new, it was probably
a bright royal blue, the same color
tag that Mabel had worn when she
was a puppy. Tess slid her finger
over the name etched in the
metal.

Suddenly, Tess's lungs refused
to produce air, her surroundings
blurred like a watercolor painting
and the waves from the lake went

completely silent. The tag only had one name etched on it, Tom.

Tess fell back, bracing herself with her slender tanned arm. She bit her lip hard. Tom had always joked that when he died, he was going to come back to this life as a Golden Retriever. But it couldn't be. She looked at the tag again, flipping it over in search of a phone number or another name that would identify the dog but there was nothing, just Tom.

Tess held the matted fur behind the dog's ears and pulled his face to her cheek. She lowered her head as the tears began to fill her eyes. She knew in her head that it was completely irrational, but in that moment, her heart took over and let her, just for a moment, believe that this dog was a sign from her husband, sent there to check up on her and make sure she was okay.

The deep sound of the dog's bark in her ear startled Tess and she snapped back to reality, dismissing her crazy thoughts. She wiped her eyes and coughed to release the hard lump in her throat. "Okay, well, we need to find out where you came from and if someone is looking for you T….." she tried to call him by the name on his tag but she couldn't do it. "If it's okay with you, I'm going to call you……." She quickly tried to think of a new name. "Blue, since you have a blue tag." She knew it was a lame reason but she liked the name.

Tess gathered herself up, shook the sand from her beach towel and wrapped it around her waist. "C'mon Blue, let's go up to the Lodge and get you a drink and something to eat. Then we'll try and get you back home."

As the two walked side by side up the grass hill toward the Lodge, she felt a twinge of guilt. A part of her, the same part that wanted to believe this dog was some sort of a sign from Tom, secretly wished that the dog could stay with her at the Lodge. She and Tom had always planned on getting another dog once the renovations were completed at the Lodge but after Tom died, Tess had been too busy. She missed having a dog of her own and thought Blue might make the perfect companion. But deep down, Tess knew she had to do everything she could to find this dog's owner, for Mabel's sake.

Blue reached the back porch of the Lodge first and turned to wait for Tess. She smiled as she studied the dog's blonde coat, drying slowly under the warm morning sun. Tess gave him another pat on the head and the two hopped the steps onto the narrow back porch. Tess grabbed one of the posts with her hand and swung sideways to take another look at the lake.

"You didn't fall out of a boat out there did you, Blue? I really hope someone didn't capsize." She looked down at the dog, steadfast at her side staring out at the lake. She wished she could read his mind. "I guess I should call the police and report what happened, just in case someone out there needs help. They'll probably think I'm crazy when I tell them that you swam here from out of nowhere." Tess pulled open the screen door and patted her thigh inviting Blue to come inside.

Normally, when Tess returned from her morning swim, her route through the Lodge was swift and intentional; upstairs for a shower and a change of clothes, kitchen for a bite to eat and then off to work on whatever matter was most pressing at the Lodge. But today, her shower would have to wait. She wanted to give Blue a drink and something to eat before she did anything else.

Tess watched as the dog bounded through the Lodge with an eerie familiarity, darting past the stone fireplace and weaving his way through the Lodge dining room, heading straight for the kitchen. Tess giggled as Blue sniffed out the dog treats that she kept in the bottom corner cabinet of her rustic pine kitchen. "You need a drink and some food first and then maybe we'll talk about snacks." She was amazed at how quickly she was bonding with this mysterious dog.

She took a large metal bowl down from the cupboard and filled it with water. She placed the bowl at her feet and Blue immediately lapped up the fresh cold water. As the dog drank, Tess glanced out the window at the lake once again. What happened out there? Why did this dog come to me? Why does his tag say Tom and nothing else? None of this makes any sense. She could feel the emotions flooding to her face again as her thoughts bounced from emotional to rational – from the unknown to the here and now. She blinked hard and turned to the fridge.

"Okay boy, since I have no idea what you like to eat, I'm going to give you the same meal I offer the dogs who stay here; fresh, homemade food with real meat, rice and vegetables so you can be strong and healthy. And after the swim you had this morning, you're probably really hungry so I'm going to make you a double portion." Tess mixed up the ingredients as Blue stood contentedly at her side, drool dripping onto her bare feet.

"Here you go," Tess offered. "Now, don't gobble or you'll have a sore stomach." But her warning was lost on the hungry dog that devoured the bowl of food in a matter of seconds. Tess shook her head as she lifted the empty bowl and placed it in the sink. Blue's eyes followed her every move and Tess could tell he was quietly wishing for more. "Well, I guess you're waiting for the treats I promised, huh? Okay but just a couple." Tess crouched down and held out her hand, three small treats in her palm. Blue took them gently – careful not to hurt her – and then proceeded to crunch them so violently that a puddle of crumbs and slobber formed on the floor around his paws. Tess tossed her head back and laughed.

As Blue licked up the biscuit crumbs, Tess heard the familiar sound of a car approaching on the rough gravel road leading to the Lodge. "That can't be a guest yet," Tess glanced at the clock. "It's only eight o'clock. Check-in isn't until nine." Tess walked out to the front window to see who was coming.

Beckett Lodge was the only property on Murray Lake Road, so whenever Tess heard a car, either someone was coming to the Lodge or they were lost. Tess remembered their realtor's warning about how secluded this place was. He insisted that visitors to the Lodge would hate being 40 miles away from the nearest town and its amenities. She found his advice amusing. The whole idea of a vacation Lodge was for people to get away from their everyday life, to be still and quiet for a change. Besides, the nearest town, Kilter Falls, and its "amenities" were about as much fun as a country love song.

As the growl of the gravel got louder, Tess could see that it was Max's truck, a familiar sight around the Lodge.

Max Sharpley owned the bait and tackle shop in Kilter Falls and he and Tom had become fast friends after they bought the Lodge. Before Tom died, the two spent countless hours on the lake fishing, and Max was always on-hand to help with any Lodge renovations. He loved Tess's home cooking and there was always a plate set for him at the dining room table. When Tom died, Max was there to help Tess pick up the pieces. He handled things at the Lodge, did her shopping and helped with the funeral arrangements. Looking back, Tess wondered how she would have gotten through any of it without him.

Max didn't come around as often as he had when Tom was alive but he still came out to the Lodge at least once a week to check in on her. She told him over and over that it wasn't necessary, that she was fine, but he came anyway.

Tess opened the front screen door and stepped onto the wiry welcome carpet with her bare feet, Blue still glued to her side. She watched Max as he stepped out of his truck wearing his familiar cargo shorts and loose-fitting button up shirt. Whenever she saw Max, she couldn't help but think of Tom. They were quite a pair, joking and laughing - like brothers- and just the sight of Max made Tess feel comfortable and happy.

"Hey, Max. Your truck could use a wash!" She joked, as if trying to fill Tom's brotherly-like shoes.

"Why do you think I'm here? You can squeeze that in before your next guest arrives, can't you?" He joked and hopped up onto the covered porch.

Max noticed that Tess was still wearing her bathing suit, towel around her waist, tousled curly hair still wet and clinging to her shoulders. He knew she swam each morning but had never seen her in anything less than long shorts and a tank top. *God she was beautiful.* He had always thought so. Ever since the first time he saw her, standing in his tackle shop, asking him about fishing lures. She was naturally beautiful, the type of woman that didn't need make-up or fancy clothes to look good. If she hadn't been married, she was exactly the type of woman Max would be interested in. But she was married...to a man he considered his best friend.

Max glanced down at the dog standing by Tess's side, "Well, who do we have here?" He reached down and stroked the dog's blonde coat. Blue wagged his tail and raised his head to Max's hand.

"Well..." Tess paused, trying to find the right words. "I was sitting on the beach this morning and he just appeared, swimming in from the lake. Did you hear anything on the radio about a boating accident?" Tess certainly wasn't going to tell Max about the dog's name tag and how emotional it had made her. Max would think she was a raving lunatic.

"No, I didn't hear about anything but when I get back to town, I'll call Dan down at the station and see if anything has been reported. I'll let you know. What are you going to do with him in the meantime? He has a tag here."

Before Tess could say anything, Max crouched down to have a look at the dog's faded blue tag. "Huh, it just says Tom. That's odd." Max paused and Tess wondered what he was thinking, waiting to hear what he said next. "That's going to make it hard to find his owner," he shrugged.

Tess let out the breath she hadn't realized she was holding. Of course, Max wouldn't think the dog was anything more than a stray and his inspection of the tag and lack of reaction made Tess realize how silly it was for her to think so either. It was just a dog with a careless owner, nothing more.

"I call him Blue, suits him better than Tom." Tess knelt down and rubbed the fur under the dog's chin. "I'm going to call the animal shelter and the vet right away in case someone has left word there and then, once my guests are settled in, I'll head into town and ask around, see if anyone recognizes him. He's a good dog. I kind of like having him around but I hate to think someone might be missing him." She stood and looked at Max. "Do you want to stay for breakfast?"

"Sorry, I can't today Tess. Can I take a rain check?" His soft brown eyes looked at her like a child waiting to be forgiven. He would have loved nothing more than to stay and be with her, but he had a supplier stopping into the shop in a few hours.

"You know you're welcome anytime. And you know; you don't have to……"

"Now, don't start. You know the only reason I come out here is so you'll feel sorry for me, lonely bachelor that I am and feed me some good nutritious food." Max turned and stepped down from the porch. "A man can't survive on canned beans and macaroni alone you know?" He called over his shoulder. They both laughed as

Max pulled himself into his truck. Tess liked it when he hid his protective intentions. As the truck pulled away, Tess waved and yelled, "See ya!"

"Well, Blue. I better go and get dressed. The guests will be arriving any minute."

But as Tess turned to open the screen door, Blue bolted from the porch onto the gravel road, chasing Max's truck.

"Hey! Come back!" Tess screamed as she leapt from the porch. "Blue…. Tom…. No! You're going to get lost out there, come back!" Tess ran after the dog, the gravel cutting into her bare feet. She watched helplessly as the dog started to fade from her sight. He stopped briefly and looked back at her, as if to say goodbye. Then the dog rounded the corner and disappeared from Tess's view. Winded, she slumped over and put her hands on her knees, staring at the bend in the road, hoping to see the dog reappear. "Please come back."

Tess just stood there, in the middle of the road, pondering the events of the morning and talking to herself out loud. "A dog appears from out of nowhere, with Tom's name etched on his dog tag, makes me question my sanity, steals my heart and then leaves as quickly as he came. It was silly to think he was any kind of…. anything; he's was just a lost dog."

But try as she might, her head simply couldn't convince her heart.

She turned back toward the Lodge, glancing over her shoulder every few steps hoping to see Blue running back to her. But he never came. As she reached the porch, she waited for a few moments before heading inside.   She wanted to jump in her car and chase after the dog, to bring him back, but she needed to get dressed and be ready when her guests arrived. Business was business. As she took one last peek down the road, Tess felt thankful for the brief time she got to spend with Blue and hoped he would find a safe place to stay.

Tess had barely finished getting ready when her first guest arrived. She flew down the stairs and made her way to the front entrance. She crept to the window and inched back the curtain, stealing a quick glimpse at who would be spending the week at the Lodge. She swallowed hard as a tall, impossibly handsome man stepped out of his truck. His long plaid shorts and wrinkled T-shirt did little to hide his impressive physique and his short brown hair was sun-kissed and windblown. She watched as he lifted a large German Shepherd down from the passenger side, obviously old and unable to jump. She felt a twinge of sadness as she pulled herself away from the window and into the front lobby. Tess pushed open the screen door and held it open for her new guests.

"Hi there, you must be James," she watched as the handsome stranger guided his elderly pet up the three wooden steps onto the porch.

"No actually my name is Brandon, Brandon Bishop. James is my boss. He made the reservation for me; I hope that's alright?"

"Oh, of course, that's no problem, c'mon in." Tess held out her hand to the stately Shepherd so he could give her an accepting sniff. "Your dog is beautiful, what's his name?"

"This is Toto," Brandon answered shyly.

"Oh, I love the Wizard of Oz, it's one of my favorite movies" Tess knelt and stroked the Shepherds head. "But you don't look anything like *that* Toto." The minute she said it, Tess knew it sounded stupid and was probably something Brandon heard all the time.

"He's a K-9, my law enforcement partner in Swallowdale, we track missing people and get them home," Brandon explained. "That's why they named him Toto."

"Wow, a police dog. I'm not sure we've ever had a dog so dignified here at the Lodge. Are you both here to enjoy some time away from the action?" Tess turned as the three made their way to the small antique table in the front lobby where Tess kept all of the Lodge information. She had welcomed plenty of guests over the past few years but none had made her feel as nervous as she felt right now. Tess tried to stay composed; it would be bad for business if she acted like a giddy school girl in front of her handsome guest.

"Yep, we just needed a little break. Just wrapped up a pretty intense case, that……" Brandon paused and stuttered, "Didn't end well, so my boss figured I needed some time off to get my head back in the game. And Toto here is getting pretty old and nearing retirement so we're looking forward to kicking back and enjoying a little rest and relaxation this week."

"Well, you've certainly come to the right place."

As Tess told Brandon about the amenities at the Lodge, she found it difficult to look at him. His piercing blue eyes were almost hypnotizing and his ridiculously handsome smile, framed perfectly by his rugged unshaven jaw line, made her knees feel weak.

"You guys are staying in Rosseau Cottage which is our cabin just to the right of the main Lodge. You can go out the back door, just through here, and follow the pathway. That'll lead you right to the front door. You should have everything you need in the cabin but if there is anything else, you'd like, please don't hesitate to let me know. Dinner is served every night here at the main Lodge at 7:00 if you'd like to come and

Toto is more than welcome to join us." Tess breathed a sigh of relief as she finished her canned flight-attendant-like speech.

"Sounds great," Brandon smiled and Tess absorbed every second of it. "We'll be here."

As Brandon and Toto made their way to the cabin, Tess felt excited in a way she hadn't for a long time. She felt the same way she did the first time she saw Tom, standing next to her in line at the county fair. She lowered her head as the memories of Tom made her think about Blue again. She wished he hadn't run off like he did. She wanted more time to figure it all out. She wanted to know where he had come from and who he belonged to. Now she would never know.

Tess was busy in the kitchen prepping the food for the day when she heard a woman's voice call from the lobby. She quickly weaved her way to the front of the Lodge yelling her apologies. "I'm so sorry; I didn't hear you pull up."

As Tess approached from the hallway, she could tell the woman was not impressed. "We're here to check in, reservation for Joanne Lawrence," the woman snapped.

Judging by how the woman was dressed, Tess figured she was

used to first-class service and nothing less. Jewelry dripped from her ears, neck and wrists and her gold rimmed handbag probably cost more than Tess's entire wardrobe. She was dressed entirely in black and her platinum blonde hair was cut into a perfect triangular wedge. Tess glanced down at her stilt-like stilettos and hoped she had packed some other, more appropriate, footwear.

"Of course, Mrs. Lawrence, welcome to Beckett Lodge," Tess knew it was too late to impress her but offered a friendly smile anyway. Tess continued, "You are staying in Clearwater Cottage …." but was cut short by the ring of the woman's cell phone.

"I have to take this," she boasted and turned her back.

Tess smiled at the little boy who had been hiding behind his mother. He was purely adorable with crooked wire-rimmed glasses and a faded blue baseball cap. Tess could tell he was shy so she knelt down to talk to him. "Hi there, what's your name?" she whispered, trying not to interrupt his mother's important phone call.

"Gavin," the boy replied.

"Hi Gavin, my name's Tess. Welcome to Beckett Lodge. Did you bring your dog with you?"

"Yes. He's waiting in the car. Mommy says he's too big to come in here. He's a Saint Bernard."

"Oh my, he must be big then. I can't wait to meet him. What's his name?"

"Derby."

"That's a great name. Are you and Derby excited to be on vacation?"

"Yeah. Mommy will be busy doing work and stuff so me and Derby are going to make sandcastles and swim at the beach."

"That sounds perfect. I hope you and Derby have a really good time while you're here," Tess stood just as Joanne was wrapping up her phone call.

After a snide remark about how lousy the cell service was and no apologies for her abrupt interruption, Joanne told Tess to continue.

"Clearwater Cottage is going to be your home away from home for the week and its right over here to the left of the main Lodge." Tess stretched her finger out to her side. "Just follow the flagstone pathway right up to the door. Have a look around and if there's anything you need, please let me know. I serve dinner here in the Lodge dining room at 7:00, a nice home cooked meal if you'd like to join us." Tess bent over and spoke directly to Gavin, "and

Derby can come too, I'll cook him an extra special meal." Tess winked at the boy who smiled and quickly looked to his mother for approval.

"Not tonight, Gavin. I have a lot to do, so I think we'll just make something in the cabin." The boy hung his head and tried not to cry. "Let's go, I need to make another phone call." Joanne repositioned her handbag on her shoulder and grabbed for the little boy's hand.

"We have to get Derby," Gavin sobbed with urgency as he and his mother turned to leave the Lodge.

"How could we forget him?" the woman snarled at the boy sarcastically.

Tess watched the two make their way to the car and her heart felt heavy for the little boy. It was obvious his mother would rather be anywhere but here. Tess wondered what her story was, why she seemed so angry and resentful about being here and why she had such obvious distaste for their St. Bernard.

Tess was in awe of the dog's size as he leapt from the car. He was a cumbersome but beautiful animal. She smiled as she watched Gavin and the dog together. They were like beauty and the beast, standing eye to eye beside the car. Gavin giggled as Derby licked his face like an ice cream cone melting on a hot summer day, something Tess was sure his mother probably despised.

The three eventually made their way down the path to the cabin. Tess couldn't hear Joanne's voice as they walked away but she was certain the woman was complaining about how uneven the trail was as she paraded her assortment of rolling suitcases and oversized bags down the hand laid stones in her stilettos. Tess chuckled out loud as Joanne swatted away an army of bugs who found her perfume more fragrant than the gardens. It was going to be a long week.

With both of her guests checked in and happily spending the day becoming familiar with the Lodge, Tess's thoughts turned back to Blue. Even though he had run away, she still wanted to find out where he had come from and whether anyone was looking for him. She made a few calls, one to the animal shelter in town and one to the vet. Neither was aware of anyone looking for a lost Retriever and neither knew anyone named Tom that may be the dog's owner. Tess also called the police station and reported what had happened. They had no accident reports from the lake and no one had called to report a lost dog. They told Tess it wasn't necessary for her to file a report either as long as she and the dog were both safe. They took her information and said they would call if they heard anything. Tess felt strangely relieved. Maybe she wasn't crazy after all. Maybe this mysterious encounter was more than just a random coincidence. Tess shook her head and shrugged. None of it made any sense so she decided to quit thinking about it. Blue was gone and apparently there was no one looking for him so it was time to forget the whole thing ever happened and get on with what needed to be done around the Lodge.

Tess filled the day with typical chores; weeded the massive gardens, topped-up the bird feeders, replaced a light bulb on the back patio and washed the pontoon boat. And even though she had promised herself not to, she secretly thought about Blue and hoped he was safe, wherever he was. She also thought about Tom and her new guests and her crazy life in general. Oddly, she felt blessed to have the life she did. It was challenging and a bit lonely without Tom by her side, but life at the Lodge was good.

Throughout the day Tess caught glimpses of her new guests out and about at the Lodge. Brandon and Toto spent the majority of the day enjoying short walks on the trails and fishing from the dock. She admired the obvious bond the two shared, a quiet protection between dog and master. She knew if it came down to it, whether it was in the line of duty or not, one would gladly take a bullet for the other. They were beautiful together.

As for the Lawrence clan in the other cabin, things didn't seem to be going as smoothly. Joanne, flustered and hurried, usually with a cell phone to her ear and a permanently furrowed brow, seemed constantly irritated. Gavin and Derby on the other hand, looked as happy as clams frolicking on the beach together. Derby was a gentle giant who attentively followed the little boy everywhere - except when Gavin was swimming in the lake. Then Derby paced the beach, back and forth, his eyes never straying from the boy in the small red life jacket. They too, were a beautiful pair.

As the sun slowly sank behind the tips of the tall trees, Tess made her way to the Lodge to get cleaned up and begin preparing for dinner. Her stomach fluttered when she remembered that Brandon and Toto were the only ones who accepted her dinner invitation. Normally, she loved to join her guests in the dining room and get to know them a little, make them feel like family. But she wondered whether Brandon Bishop would rather eat alone; he obviously had things on his mind. Or perhaps he could use someone to talk to. Either way, she was excited about seeing the handsome police officer again.

Once she had dinner in the oven, Tess hurried upstairs to have a shower and change her clothes. The top soil stains on her knees and her old Michigan State tank top were certainly not going to impress any dinner guest. She wanted to look nice but not over the top and she certainly didn't want to wear something that screamed *I haven't been this excited about a man in a long time!* She opted for a blue floral sun dress, simple and pretty.

Tess floated down the stairs into the dining room, her cascade of brunette curls bouncing atop her shoulders. She smiled as the setting sun lit the room with a warm glow. Tess paused in front of the huge stone fireplace. Sometimes in the summer, rather than a fire, she would light a cluster of simple white pillar candles on the hearth to add some warmth to the dining room. But tonight, was different. She didn't want the dining room to look romantic, like she and Brandon were on a date, so opted not to light the candles and turned the wall sconces on instead.

Content with how the evening was shaping up so far, Tess popped into the kitchen to check on the food. As she reached to the cabinet for serving dishes, she saw the unwashed bowl from Blue's morning meal, still sitting in the sink. She lowered her hands and gazed out the window toward the lake. The waves were still and the water was getting dark. She hoped Blue had found shelter before dark.

If there was one thing Brandon Bishop was looking forward to on his first day at Beckett Lodge, it was the home cooked meal he was promised. Back at home, his meals usually consisted of stale, leftover sandwiches or quick bites made in the microwave. Unless of course, his mother was visiting, then he was fed enough food for thirty men.

Brandon called to Toto, "Well, old friend, should we make our way to the Lodge for some food? I'm starving." Brandon looked at his watch to be sure they were going to be on time.

Toto sat at Brandon's feet and looked up at him, his head slightly tilted at the mention of food. Even though he was getting old, he still liked to eat and Tess had promised him a delicious meal as well.

Brandon sat down on the edge of the bed and slipped on his Reeboks. It was these insignificant moments of silence when Brandon found himself thinking about the Porchman case and wondering if he would ever be able to forgive himself. They were so close to finding that little girl, unfairly close, but they didn't. She died in a musty old basement while he and Toto were rummaging through the neighbors shed looking for her. Brandon wished he could mute the tiny nagging voice in his heart that told him maybe everyone was right, maybe Toto was getting too old to do his job and it was time for him to train a new, younger dog with a better nose. No. He wasn't ready to give up on Toto.

Brandon quickly finished tying his shoe and raised himself up from the bed. He studied the big dog, so noble and majestic. Brandon knew Toto had saved his ass on more than one occasion and his chest ached when he thought about their partnership coming to an end. He knelt down and hugged Toto.

Toto leaned into Brandon's body, *I know, Boss. I feel the same way about you. But I am tired and slow and soon it will be my time to leave you. I just hope, before I go, that you can forgive me for*

*not leading you to that little girl
and trust that I didn't let you
down. I would never let you
down.*

"C'mon Toto, let's go."

The two faithful friends left their
cabin at the edge of the woods
and headed to the Lodge for
dinner. Brandon walked slowly
beside the dog, guiding him down
the stone pathway. Toto's limp
seemed to be getting worse and
Brandon wondered if his hips were
causing him pain.

"Just a bit further and then you
can rest," Brandon reassured the

dog. "And let's hope this woman can cook," he whispered, "We sure could use a good meal, eh boy?" Toto looked up at him and Brandon was sure he agreed.

Tess looked up at the clock as it chimed and tip toed to the window. She didn't want Brandon Bishop to see her looking for him if he was already on his way to the Lodge. She pulled back the curtain and glanced down the pathway. No sign of Brandon or Toto. Puzzled she looked toward the Lawrence cabin. If Brandon wasn't going to come for dinner, she hoped that maybe Joanne Lawrence had changed her mind and would bring her little boy over to the Lodge instead. She had made a lot of food to eat all by herself.

As Tess peeked through the window, she could see Gavin and Derby happily playing on the grass in front of the cabin. They were running in circles, Gavin with a towel tied around his neck like a cape, and Derby following his every move. Tess figured Gavin was probably pretty good at entertaining himself while his mother was busy making and taking important phone calls. Tess pressed her forehead closer to the window to look for

Joanne. Surprisingly, she wasn't on the phone at all. She was sitting on the porch swing, reading, and for once she actually looked comfortable and content. Maybe, Tess thought, Joanne Lawrence was going to enjoy her stay here at the Lodge after all.

"Is this the right place for dinner?"

Tess jumped and spun around. Brandon was standing outside the screen door, looking in. She hoped he hadn't seen her spying on her guests.

"It sure is, c'mon in." Tess pushed the screen door open and invited them into the dining room. "Hi, Toto," she bent down and scratched the dog on the back of his neck. "How did you guys enjoy your first day?"

"So far, so good, mostly just walked around the trails and enjoyed the view. Your property here is pretty incredible."

"Thank you. We have lots of trails and I always warn my guests to try and stick to them, otherwise it can be really easy to get lost out there. We have over 200 acres and with no other properties on this road, there aren't many landmarks to follow."

"Well I don't think Toto here will be exploring any hard terrain anyway, not with his hips."

"I noticed he has a bit of a limp. How old is he?" Tess led Brandon to the table as they chatted.

"He's nine, almost ten. I've had him since he was 6 months old."

The three walked toward the long wooden harvest table in the center of the dining room. Tess dragged her hand along the pitted edges of her husband's handy work. It felt like yesterday that they had argued about how to set up the dining room at the Lodge. Tom wanted to make three round tables, two for the guests and one for them, but Tess insisted on one large table where everyone could sit together and share a meal.   As was usually the case, she had won the argument and as an apology for being so stubborn, Tom made her this table. He used pine from the property and worked tirelessly for weeks to make it just right. He even carved their initials into the center of the table to remind her how much he loved her.

Tess grinned as she motioned for Brandon to have a seat. "Since you are the only guest for dinner tonight, you get the whole table to yourself, sit wherever you like."

"Your other guests aren't coming?" Brandon asked.

"Nope, not tonight, I'm afraid it is just you and Toto."

"Uh, you and your......husband?" he paused. "You won't be joining me?" Brandon questioned.

Tess was caught off guard by the question and stuttered, "No, uh, actually, my husband died 2 years ago."

"Oh, I'm sorry." Brandon shook his head and blushed slightly as he looked at her.

"But I'd be happy to join you...... if you're sure you want company." Tess smiled and tried to lighten the mood.

"Of course, I'd love to hear more about the Lodge."

"Great, then have a seat and I'll go get us the first course."

Tess headed into the kitchen as Brandon pulled out a chair and Toto clumsily laid himself at his owner's feet. Brandon studied the dining room and spotted a picture of Tess on the wall across from him. She was sitting in the grass, her knees pulled to her chest with a coy please-don't-take-my-picture smile. Her curly hair tangled around her shoulders with a bronze tan as deep as her eyes. She looked beautiful and happy.

"That was one of my husband's favorite pictures of me." Tess said as she returned to the table. "I begged him not to put it on the wall but he did it anyway. I think he actually used crazy glue when he mounted it so I wouldn't take it down." Tess laughed as she served them each a bowl of fresh garden salad.

"He was right to hang it. It's a really nice picture of you." Brandon commented.

Tess blushed, "Thanks. He took that picture just after we bought the Lodge. We had a lot of fun fixing this place up… some great memories."

"What made you two decide to open a Lodge?" Brandon asked.

"Well, we wanted a place where people could come on vacation without having to leave their dog behind. We left our dog at a kennel once while we were in the Caribbean and we never saw her again. She escaped; it was awful."

"You never found her?" Brandon asked as he unfolded his napkin.

"No. But it wasn't for lack of trying. We spent every minute looking for her. We plastered the city with flyers, we called vets and shelters, we drove around calling for her, but we never found her." Tess bowed her head.

"But hey," Tess continued, "at least one good thing came out of losing her," she raised her hands toward the ceiling and shrugged. "She was our inspiration for opening this place." She smiled at Brandon and stabbed at her salad. "But that's enough about me. I want to hear about you and Toto and your exciting police work. You said you help find missing people? That must be a tough job sometimes."

"It can be. But other times, times when we find a kid and reunite them with their parent, that's amazing. You should see Toto at work, it's......well, I guess I should say, was, something else. He's getting older and it's getting tougher for him to do that kind of work anymore."

"I saw him limping earlier when the two of you were walking. I guess he has trouble with his hips?"

"Yeah, I think they are really starting to cause him some pain. But he never quits." Brandon lovingly looked down at his dog.

"I bet he is real protective of you. I miss having a dog of my own around here. Tom and I always planned on getting one after Mabel disappeared but then we started all the work on the Lodge and just never got around to it. But I have different dogs coming and going around here all the time, so it's alright."

"It's pretty obvious you are a dog person," Brandon remarked. "I bet when you were a little girl you were always the one bringing home stray animals, right?"

"How'd you guess?" Tess and Brandon both laughed. "And it didn't stop when I was little either. Just this morning I found a stray and brought him up here." Tess's smile straightened a little as she thought of Blue. She stood and quickly changed the subject. "But then he took off again. Now, how 'bout I get us some real food. I'm sure this did nothing to satisfy your appetite." Tess pointed to the salad and began collecting their plates.

"The salad was delicious, thank you."

As Tess scooped up his plate Brandon noticed she no longer wore her wedding ring. He couldn't help but feel sorry for her. It must be a lot of work to run this place all alone. But he admired her strength and resiliency and as she walked away, he thought about how nice she looked in her sundress.

"Derby, I'm the superhero so you have to be the bad guy." Gavin, with a towel still tied around his neck, told his gigantic playmate as the two raced around on the grass in front of the cabin.

"Gavin, only a few more minutes and then we're going to get you cleaned up for bed. It's almost 8:00 and it'll be dark soon," his mother called from the porch swing.

She placed her glass of wine on the table and put her head back on the cushion. She wanted to get through these divorce papers one more time before she called it a night but her eyes were heavy. She took one more look at her son and his beast, and closed her eyes, just for a moment.

"Derby! Look! Did you see that? It was a black panther, here to destroy the universe, let's get 'em!" The little boy raised his stick like a sword and raced after a tiny black squirrel that fled into the woods. Derby followed the youngster but stopped as the boy climbed down some steep moss-covered rocks at the side of the cabin. He barked. *Don't go down there Gavin. You might get lost if you don't stay close to the cabin. Please come back, you're not safe down there.*

The lumbering Saint Bernard turned and stepped toward the cabin where Joanne Lawrence was sitting and barked again, trying to alert the sleeping woman that her son was in danger. She didn't move. Instinctively, Derby knew he needed to get to the little boy and keep him safe. He galloped back to the top of the mossy rocks, looking for Gavin at the bottom. The boy was running further into the woods, still chasing the squirrel. Derby barked again, begging him to stop, but the boy ignored his warning. Derby had no choice. He carefully made his way down the precipitous drop and ran after Gavin.

Once he reached him, Derby stood in front, nudging the boy's tiny frame back toward the cabin. But the boy was lost in make believe and untied his towel cape.

"You wear the cape now Derby," the boy instructed as he tied the blue plush towel around the dog's neck. "Let's pretend we're in Africa and we have to fight all of the wild animals. Do you think there are any lions in here? I already got one black panther!" Gavin started walking again, further and further from the cabin. Panicked, Derby tried running in the opposite direction, back the way they came, hoping the spirited child would follow. But the boy's imagination had taken over. Derby turned and caught up to the boy again, intent on keeping him safe.

Derby stayed close to the little boy as they weaved their way through the darkening woods, low slung branches whipping across Derby's face. *This is not a safe place for us to be Gavin. We need to go back. I won't leave you but please turn around.*

Derby was somewhat relieved when the boy finally stopped running, now they could start heading back to the cabin. But Gavin was scared now, realizing he had ventured a little too far into the woods and he began to cry, tears creeping down his reddened cheeks.   He dropped to his knees and clung to the big dog's neck. Derby could feel his tiny hands shaking with fright as he sobbed. Derby gently rested his muzzle atop the boy's head. *Don't worry Gavin; I'm going to get you home. Everything is going to be okay, don't cry.*

Derby knew he had to get Gavin back to the cabin but they had walked so far and everything in the woods looked the same. Derby was not used to this kind of terrain. Back home in the city, his walks consisted of a lap around the block, a visit to the park down the street and a quick jaunt around the corner to the bagel shop with Gavin and his mom. He had certainly never experienced anything like this.

Through the trees, Derby could see the tiny sliver of sky turning from midnight blue to black, the setting sun no longer reflecting through the timbers. He put his nose to the ground to try and pick up a scent, anything that could get them back to where Joanne Lawrence sat sleeping in her porch swing. But it was useless.

Then Derby heard a familiar sound. It was a car and Derby could tell it wasn't far away. He growled and whined to get Gavin's attention and when the boy stood, he started walking in the direction of the sound. Gavin wrapped his small hand around the big dog's collar, trusting that his faithful friend could lead him home.

Tess knew she should feel guilty but she didn't. She was thankful that Joanne Lawrence had decided not to accept her invitation for dinner tonight. She was enjoying having dinner with Brandon – just the two of them. He was a little quiet for her taste but he was also kind and funny and *oh* so enjoyable to look at. She smiled to herself as she returned to the dining room and asked Brandon if he'd like some dessert.

"I'm not sure if I can fit anything else in here," Brandon sighed as he arched his back and slid his hand over his stomach.

"Sure you can. You don't want to miss out on my Lemon Meringue pie, do you? It won a blue ribbon at the Kilter Falls County Fair last year." Tess teased.

"Really? Well, alright then. I don't want to leave here saying that I passed up the chance to try the locals favorite pie."

"Great. I'll go get us a slice."

Tess leaned across the table to grab Brandon's plate. In her nervous haste, she knocked his wine glass over and spilled it onto the table. Brandon jumped up and reached for his napkin, laying it down to stop the wine from reaching the floor. Tess apologized for her clumsiness as the two stood face to face, leaning over the center of the table. Brandon awkwardly continued to mop up the wine as Tess tried to hide her shy smile.

"Tess?" a voice called from the lobby. "You here?"

Startled, Tess jumped back from the edge of the table just as Max

Sharpley stepped into the dining room.

"Uh, hey Tess," Max could tell he had just interrupted something. "You still eatin' dinner?" Max shot a look at Brandon. Normally, Max was quick to offer a friendly welcome and a handshake to Tess's guests but he felt differently tonight. The wine glasses, the table set for two and Tess looking completely irresistible in her sundress, made Max uncomfortable. This looked like a date.

"Max? What are you doing here?"

But before he could answer, Blue came bounding around the corner from behind him. "Blue!" Tess screamed. "Oh my God, you're back!" She ran to the dog and crouched down to greet him, grabbing the fur behind his ears and pulling his golden muzzle to her cheek. "I thought you were gone." Tess tried to contain her emotions in front of the two men, but neither of them really understood what this dog meant to her. She lovingly stroked the dog's fur and hugged his neck. Blue fell into her, enjoying the affection.

"I guess you're happy to see him," Max said as Tess rose to her feet and tried to conceal her teary eyes.

"Yeah, I mean, I'm surprised. I thought he was gone. Where did you find him?"

"I didn't find him, he found me. He came to the shop this afternoon and hung around until my suppliers left, and then went and jumped in the back of my truck. I took him with me on a few errands and brought him back here. When did he run away?"

"Right after you left this morning, he ran off, like he was chasing you. I didn't figure I'd ever see him again."

"Well it looks like you're both pretty happy to be reunited," Max pointed to the dog who was affectionately pressing his body into Tess's legs.

"Oh, gosh, where are my manners? Max, this is Brandon Bishop and his dog Toto," Tess pointed to the German Shepherd, still sleeping at the foot of

Brandon's chair seemingly unaffected by all the commotion. "They are staying here for the week. Brandon this is Max, one of my dearest friends." Tess tucked her hand around Max's arm and squeezed.

Brandon extended his hand, "Nice to meet you." Max accepted and the two exchanged a friendly handshake. Brandon turned back to the table, "I should really call it a night. Dinner was delicious Tess, thank you." He called for Toto and waited as the dog carefully lifted himself to his feet.

Suddenly, the wooden screen door leading to the Lodge dining room swung open and Joanne Lawrence tumbled through the doorway. She looked awful. Her normally immaculate hair was tangled and tucked behind her ears and her clothes were dirty and hanging from her body. The woman tried to catch her breath as she stepped into the dim light of the dining room. Tess knew there was something terribly wrong. She could see the panic on the Joanne's mascara smeared face.

"Joanne! Are you okay? What happened? Is it Gavin? Where's Gavin?" Tess ran to the woman and held her by the shoulders.

Joanne still out of breath and crying gasped, "He's gone. I can't find him. Please help me find my little boy." Overcome with fear, Joanne collapsed to the ground. Tess knelt beside her, clutching the woman's shoulder. But it did little to comfort her. Tess looked up at Max and Brandon who had gathered in front of Joanne.

"It's her little boy. He's only five." Tess explained to the men. "Okay Joanne," Tess leaned in closer to the distraught woman and asked, "when did you see him last and where was he?" Tess knew they had to act quickly if they were going to find Gavin. It was completely dark now and if he had wandered into the woods, or gone down by the lake, they had to find him fast.

Joanne Lawrence could barely speak. "He was playing," she whispered. "I didn't mean to."

"You didn't mean to what?" Tess asked urgently.

"Fall asleep," Joanne guiltily buried her face in her hands and fell into Tess.

"It's okay Joanne. We're going to find him," Tess reassured her as she stood to talk to Max and Brandon. "We should probably check the beach first; make sure he's not down by the water. Do you want to split up and look for him?" Tess was starting to tremble as she looked toward Brandon. "What is the best plan Brandon?" calling on his expertise.

Brandon knelt in front of Joanne and spoke to her; his words were more disciplinary than Tess'. "Joanne, you have to listen to me. I am a police officer and part of my job is finding missing kids. But for me to do that, I need you to stop crying and help me, okay? Can you do that?"

Joanne lifted her head and wiped her eyes. She looked at Brandon and nodded.

"Okay, now, where was the last place you saw your son?"

"He was playing with the dog in front of the cabin. They were playing superheroes."

"What was he wearing?" Brandon asked.

"Green striped shorts, an orange t-shirt and white sandals. And he had a blue and white towel around his neck that he was using as a cape." Joanne's chin quivered as she spoke.

"Great. How long do you think he has been gone?"

"I told him he could only play for five more minutes because it was getting dark. It was almost eight o'clock, that's his bedtime. Then I.........."

Brandon sensed the woman was about to fall apart again, so he quickly asked his last question. "You said he was playing with the dog. Is the dog missing too?"

"I think so. I haven't seen him."

"What's the dog's name?"

"Derby."

Brandon stood and turned to Tess and Max. Tess had already gathered every flashlight she could find. He spoke quietly, "Toto and I will head into the woods at the side of their cabin. You both head down to the beach first and search there. Let's hope this little boy is with his dog – a Saint Bernard, right?"

Tess nodded, "And from what I saw today, that dog never leaves the little boy's side. I'm sure he's with Gavin."

"That's a really good thing right now," Brandon stated. "Okay, let's go." Brandon ran to the door and whistled for Toto. The dog was immediately at his side; as if he knew there was work to be done.

"I'm coming with you," Joanne jumped to her feet and chased after Brandon and Toto.

"Okay but we have to move fast and I need you to keep it together," Brandon called over his shoulder to her as they raced across the porch, Toto leading the way.

Tess didn't hear Joanne's response as she watched the two of them leap from the porch steps, but she felt confident that the hysterical woman was in good hands with Brandon leading the rescue. Max pulled her arm, an imperative reminder, "Beach, let's go."

The two barreled down to the beach in search of any sign of Gavin and his dog. Tess prayed that they wouldn't find anything down there. As horrible as the woods would be for a scared five-year-old boy, the deep dark water of the lake would be far worse.

The flashlight's yellow glare lit up the sand as Max scanned the beach. He called for the little boy as loud as he could as he and Tess both stopped, hopeful for a response. But the only sound was the waves gently lapping at the shore.

"I'll go this way," Tess told him, her feet pressing into the cool sand as she marched in the opposite direction.

In all of the chaos, Tess hadn't noticed that Blue was right on her heels, helping in the search. She looked down at him, the glow of the flashlight reflecting off his golden coat. Again, she wondered if Blue was sent to her for a reason. Maybe he was here to help her find this little boy.

Once she was sure she was out of Max's view, she knelt in the sand and pulled Blue close to her. She pressed her lips to the dog's fleecy ear and whispered, "I don't know if you are…. special, or…. if you're…. I don't know, a sign from Tom or something," the words felt uncomfortable coming from her mouth. "But I could sure use some help tonight."

Her hands started to tremble again as she thought about the little boy with the crooked wire-rimmed glasses that she spoke to earlier that morning. "See, this little boy is missing somewhere out here and we really need to find him, so, please, if you are more than just a lost dog, this would be a really good time to show me. I want to believe." She kissed the dog's ear, stood and turned back to the edge of the lake. She tried to call out for the boy but the lump in her throat prevented the sound from escaping. She ran back toward Max.

"Anything?" she asked.

"No." Max shook his head.

As Tess shone her flashlight in his direction, she could see the look of concern on his normally jovial face. Something about seeing him like that made Tess feel frightened. She tossed herself toward him and fell into his arms. He bundled her like a child and kissed the top of her head, her curls soft on his lips. "It's going to be okay Tess. We're going to find him." Max swept her blowing hair off the side of her face and tucked it behind her ear as Blue contentedly wedged himself at their feet. "Now, let's get up to the road and search there."

Tess stepped back and stumbled as she tried to compose herself. "Yes, let's go. Maybe they've already found him."

Brandon Bishop knew what he needed to do to find Gavin Lawrence and he wasn't about to let another child die because of his mistakes. He slowed down just enough to let Joanne catch up to him as they approached the cabin where she and the little boy were staying. "Joanne, I need a piece of Gavin's clothing so Toto can pick up his scent. Run inside and grab the first thing you can find, okay? I'll wait right here, but hurry, every minute counts right now."

As the woman disappeared into the cabin, the sound of Brandon's cell phone echoed through the night. He grabbed it from his front pocket and looked at the number. It was his boss James York. Brandon quickly stuffed the phone back into his pocket just as Joanne flew out of the cabin door holding the green bathing suit that Gavin had worn earlier that day.

"Here, here is his bathing suit," she stuttered as she flung the small pair of shorts into Brandon's hand.

Brandon knelt down beside Toto and pushed the boy's shorts to his muzzle, "Okay Toto, you know what to do. We have to find this little boy." Brandon pulled the shorts away and stared right into the Shepherds deep brown eyes, "Let's do it right this time."

The dog sat perfectly still, holding his owner's stare, *Okay Boss. I will do everything I can to save this little boy and give you the redemption you need. This will be my last rescue so I'm going to give it all I've got. Got his scent, let's go.*

Brandon patted his partner on the side, stood and turned to Joanne, "Let's go find your son."

Brandon's confidence offered Joanne a glimmer of hope that Gavin would be found. She had been so selfish these last few months, so wrapped up in the divorce and her work that she had been neglecting the one thing that really mattered to her. And now he was lost and alone in the woods, without his mother to keep him safe. The guilt was eating her alive. She would never be able to forgive herself if anything happened to her little boy.

The forest was dark and thick with overgrown brush and low hanging branches. Brandon ducked and lunged as he pushed the sharp needled boughs to the side, always keeping his flashlight in front of Toto who was leading the way. As the three weaved their way through the ominous woods in search of the missing boy, Brandon couldn't help but admire Toto at work. The way he maneuvered through the forest reminded Brandon of their early training days on the agility course. He was the best in his class, and Brandon had the certificate to prove it. Some of the top K-9 trainers in the country said Toto was one of the finest they'd ever seen. Brandon thought about how special he was, then and now, as he watched the old dog pushing through the woods, nose to the ground, his limp barely noticeable. He was like a well-oiled machine when he was at work.

Brandon and Joanne continued to call for the boy, but there was no response. Suddenly, Toto took a sharp turn to his left and headed up a steep hill. Brandon wondered, just for a moment, if Toto had lost the scent. There was no way a five-year-old boy could make that climb. He hesitated and thought about the Porchman case. Toto had led him astray that night, mistakenly leading him and his fellow officers to the neighbors shed instead of the house two doors down. If Toto had gone to the right house that night, the little girl might still be alive. He questioned whether he should trust Toto's instincts and follow him up the hill ahead which was heavily congested with immense pine trees.

"Does your dog think my little boy is up there?" Brandon could hear the fear in Joanne's voice as he followed Toto with the flashlight.

Brandon certainly didn't want Joanne to know he was having doubts about his dog's ability so he quickly answered, "Yes, and he isn't usually wrong so we need to follow him up there," trying to convince himself as well.

The three carefully made their way up the hill, Brandon and

Joanne both filled with doubt that Gavin could have navigated the vertical incline. As they reached the top, they heard the faint sound of voices calling for Gavin. "It must be Tess and Max," Brandon said softly to Joanne.

"They're calling for Gavin," disappointment filled Joanne's voice, "That means they haven't found him either." Brandon could hear Joanne sobbing behind him as they caught up to Toto, still sniffing the fallen leaves scattered across the ground.

"Was the little boy here Toto?" Brandon asked desperately, hoping they hadn't gone in the wrong direction. But Toto didn't lift his muzzle. Instead he forged ahead, still tracking Gavin's scent. Brandon decided he had to trust him and called for Joanne to hurry up.

Tess and Max's voices seemed to be getting closer. Brandon yelled, "Tess! Max!"

"We're over here!" Max hollered.

Brandon turned in the direction of Max's voice and saw the faint stream of golden light from their flashlight. Toto was headed right toward them.

"We're coming your way! Toto still has Gavin's scent!" Brandon yelled.

"Okay. We're up here on the road," Max responded and turned to Tess, "Maybe the little guy made his way out to the road. Let's hope." He grabbed Tess's hand and the two stood and waited for Brandon and Joanne to emerge from the forest.

The snapping of branches and rustle of leaves as Max, Joanne and Toto appeared from the tree line was loud in Tess's ear. Normally, the forest around the Lodge was so quiet at night with only the lullaby of crickets and tree frogs filling the night air. But tonight, there was nothing peaceful about the woods and Tess was fearful. She shuddered when she thought of the tiny boy, lost in this vast, dark place. Max squeezed her hand tighter to stop her from trembling.

"Any sign of Gavin?" Max called to the dark figures as they stepped into the glow of his flashlight.

"No, but Toto still seems to have his scent. We should let him lead the way," Brandon instructed.

Tess gathered Joanne in her arms and whispered to her, "We're going to find him Joanne. I promise." Tess regretted the words as soon as they left her lips. She looked down at Blue and in her head, begged him to help.

Joanne winced and fell back from Tess.

"Joanne!" Tess yelled and grabbed the woman around the waist. Max and Brandon, who had already started up the road in search of Gavin, turned and rushed back to where the women sat, crumpled at the edge of the gravel.

"What happened?" Brandon asked Tess as he shone the flashlight toward the two women.

By then, Tess had realized that Joanne was barefoot, her feet bleeding and sore from searching the woods. "It's her feet! They're all torn up. She can't go any further."

"Yes, I can," Joanne shrieked. "I need to find my son!" But as she tried to stand, she fell back into Tess's arms, the gravel, like shards of glass, piercing the exposed flesh of her feet.

"Joanne," Tess gently turned the woman's chin toward her, "I'm going to take you back to the cabin and get you cleaned up. You can't help anyone like this." With her other hand, Tess started untying the laces of her tennis shoes. "Here put on my shoes so you can try and walk back to the cabin."

Max and Brandon helped Joanne to her feet. Tess pulled her close, wrapping her hand around Joanne's barely-there waist. "It's going to be okay, Joanne. Let's go," Tess whispered.

"Here, take my flashlight," Max offered. "Brandon and I will keep searching for Gavin. Are you sure you're okay Tess?"

"I'm fine," Tess said as she looked pleadingly at Max. They both knew she wouldn't be fine until they found that little boy. "I'll call Dan too," Tess whispered, not wanting to alert Joanne to the fact that she was going to call the Kilter Falls police station to come and help them search for the missing boy.

"C'mon Blue," Tess muttered as she and Joanne started to stagger forward. The Retriever hadn't left her side since he had returned to the Lodge and Tess wanted to keep it that way. They had already lost one of her guests to the woods tonight; she didn't want to risk losing Blue again too. But Blue didn't come when Tess called him. Instead, he turned and ran to Brandon and Max. As she watched him go, Tess prayed that he could help them find Gavin.

Max ran and caught up to Brandon who was following Toto, lighting his way with the flashlight. The old dog still had his nose to the ground as he prowled the shoulder of the winding gravel road. The men walked side by side, listening for Gavin and his dog.

Blue ran past the two men and fell in line behind Toto, staying a fair distance behind, almost as if he knew not to interrupt the dog's work. But then suddenly, Blue darted ahead of Toto and stopped, blocking the big Shepherd's path. With his nose to the forest, Blue began to bark, gently at first and then more aggressive. Toto lifted his head to accept Blue's warning and the two dogs suddenly charged back into the woods.

"Maybe they heard something," Brandon said as the two men followed the dogs into the woods.

Back at the cabin, Tess tended to Joanne's sore and swollen feet, her perfectly manicured toenails now chipped and jagged from her barefoot hike through the forest. As Tess wrapped Joanne's feet in gauze, she felt oddly proud of the woman sitting in front of her. She had stopped at nothing to save her child. And now, here she sat, bleeding and vulnerable, stripped of her big city facade. Tess much preferred her this way, but certainly not under these circumstances.

"Okay Joanne, how does that feel?" Tess looked up at Joanne as she gently placed the woman's bandaged feet on the floor. "Try standing."

Joanne put her hand on the back of the chair to brace herself as she slowly tried to stand. She gripped the chair tightly and turned away from Tess as the pain shot up her legs. Hiding her face in her hand, she began to cry, a gut-wrenching primal cry that could only come from a woman who was terrified for her child.

Tess went to her. "Joanne, I'm going to call the Kilter Falls police station. They'll send everyone they have out here to find Gavin, okay? And Brandon and Max are still searching too. We are going to find him." Tess picked up the phone and started to dial the number, wishing she didn't have to.

Just as she was about to dial the last number, Tess paused. She thought she heard something, a dog barking in the distance. Was she just wishing it to be, or were they back from the woods?

Tess turned to Joanne who had sat back down in the chair, rocking back and forth, staring blankly out the window. Tess didn't want to give her any false hope so she stayed quiet about what she had heard and crept to the screen door. As soon as Joanne saw Tess head to the door, she bolted out of the chair and was right behind her.

"What are you looking at? Did you hear something?" Joanne pushed past Tess and hobbled out onto the porch. She peered into the night, down the gravel road where they had separated from the two men. But there was nothing. No flashlights, no dogs, nothing. Joanne limped down the porch steps and into the darkness. "Gaaavvinnnn!" she cried.

Then they heard it, a faint bark and the distant sound of a man's voice, like whispers in the night.

"Maybe they have Gavin," Joanne said wishfully as she started shuffling toward the road.

"Wait, Joanne. Let me grab the flashlight." Tess ran back inside and snatched it from the table. She stopped and looked to the ceiling, praying that Max and Brandon had found the little boy.

She jumped from the porch and ran to Joanne who had stopped at the side of the road, bent at the waist, her arm wrapped around a tree. Tess knew she was in incredible pain.

"Okay Joanne, let's go," Tess locked her arm around Joanne's elbow and tried to gently pry her from the tree. But the woman didn't budge. She was frozen, paralyzed by fear.

"I can't Tess. What if they don't have him? What if he is still out there in the dark, alone…… or worse, what if he……."

Joanne pressed her exhausted body to the tree, her tear stained cheek resting on the coarse bark. Tess stood with her as they watched the road, anxiously waiting for a sign.

And then it came.

The golden beam of Brandon's flashlight broke through the dark night, guiding the men toward the Lodge. Blue was in front, leading the group, his pale coat bathed in the narrow ray of light. Tess thought the dog looked angelic in the backlit glow and prayed that he had brought them a miracle.

Tess squinted and tried to make out the next figure emerging from the shadows. It was Max and he was holding the little boy on his hip. "Oh thank God," Tess pressed her hand to her chest and turned to Joanne. "They have him Joanne. Max has Gavin." Joanne looked up but still didn't move. Tess could hear Max's voice talking to the boy and then she heard Gavin giggle. Only Max could make a scared child who had been lost in the woods for hours, feel safe enough to laugh.

Joanne straightened her limp body and took a few steps slowly toward her son. Gavin called to her and she cried, running to her son, no longer feeling the pain of her wounded feet. She tugged the boy from Max's hip and held him, wrapping her arms around his tiny frame, pressing him to her chest. She buried her face in his neck and wept as she dropped to her knees. Then she pulled him away, inspecting his face and brushing his hair off of his forehead. "Are you okay, Honey? Are you hurt?" Joanne sniffled as she traced his face with her fingers.

"I lost my glasses Mommy," Gavin said shyly.

Joanne tilted her head to the side and smiled at the boy. "That's okay sweetie. We'll get you a new pair." She pulled him close again and squeezed him tight as she stood. She looked to Max and thanked him for finding her son.

"The only thanks should go to that big dog of yours. I'm sure he did everything he could to keep Gavin safe out there. When we found them, your boy was curled up around him, sleeping like a baby. It's a good thing the dog followed him out there."

Joanne looked down at Derby, still protectively standing guard as she held Gavin. She stroked the dog's head and for the first time since the dog had come into their lives, Joanne didn't move away when he affectionately pressed his body against her legs.

"Where are Brandon and Toto?" Tess whispered to Max.

"They're a little ways back," Max pointed down the road. "The old Shepherd had to stop and take a breather. I think he overdid it out there and is hurtin' real bad."

Tess looked down the road. "I'm going to go make sure they are okay. Will you take Joanne and Gavin to the main Lodge and make sure they're both alright? I'll be right there."

"Sure thing," Max nodded as he wrapped his arm around Joanne and Gavin and guided them toward the Lodge. He looked back at Tess who was running into the darkness with Blue by her side and for a fleeting moment, wondered if Tess's concern for Brandon was more personal than professional. Either way, it was hard to watch her run off. He turned back to Joanne and Gavin and ushered the reunited pair back to the Lodge.

"Brandon?" Tess called into the dark, following the light from his lowered flashlight.

"We're right here Tess," he called back.

Tess slowed her pace to a walk when she realized that Brandon was huddled on the side of the road, protectively crouched over his dog.

"Is he okay?" Tess knelt down beside the Shepherd who was lying with his chin on the ground between his outstretched front legs.

Brandon shrugged slightly and answered, "I don't know. He can't seem to breathe very well and if he takes more than a few steps, he has to lie down and rest. I think that climb may have been too much for his old hips. I think I'll try to carry him back to our cabin."

He lovingly stroked the dog's back and assured him that it was going to be okay. Tess stood to the side as Brandon bent down and gently scooped the dog up from the shoulder of the road. The Shepherd let out a soft whimper as his master lifted him in the air.

As Brandon staggered under the weight of Toto, draped across his arms, he heard his cell phone ring again. He turned to Tess. "I'm sure that's just my boss checking in on me again. He'll have to wait." He struggled to readjust the limp dog, trying not to cause him anymore pain.

"Let me lead the way back to your cabin. Be careful," Tess cautioned.

Shining the flashlight ahead of Brandon, Tess couldn't help but feel guilty. These were her guests, here to enjoy some rest and relaxation and escape the daily grind of their day to day police work, but instead, they were sent on a grueling rescue mission that had obviously caused the old dog a great deal of pain.

"How is Gavin?" Brandon asked, slightly out of breath.

"He seems to be fine, he's with his Mom. Max took them both back to the main Lodge to get warmed up and checked out. The little guy was upset about losing his glasses."

Brandon smiled. "I'm glad he's okay. I'll go see him tomorrow."

The two walked the rest of the way in silence until they finally reached the cabin. Tess unlocked the door and pushed it open. Once inside, Brandon gently laid Toto on the soft bear skin rug that covered the floor at the foot of the bed. The dog looked very tired and was still unable to stand on his own.

"I really hope he's okay," Tess said in an apologetic tone. "I feel terrible that the two of you had to go through all of that."

"I'm glad we were here to help," Brandon mumbled, not taking his eyes off Toto.

Tess knew it was time to leave the two of them alone.

"I can't thank you enough for finding that little boy. I'm not sure what we would have done if you and Toto hadn't been here. If you need anything, for you or for Toto, please call me at the main Lodge."

Brandon looked at Tess briefly and smiled before his eyes fell back on Toto, who was already fast asleep on the rug. "Goodnight Tess. Hey, please tell Gavin I will come and see him in the morning...he's a pretty brave little boy."

"I will." Tess replied. "Goodnight". She pulled the cabin door closed behind her and headed back down the path toward the main Lodge. She stopped briefly and glanced back over her shoulder at the cabin. She could see Brandon through the small window, sitting on the edge of the bed with his head in his hands. Tess bit her lip and hoped that by morning, everything would be better.

She looked down at Blue who was becoming a permanent fixture by her side. "C'mon Blue. Let's go home."

Tess reached the main Lodge just as Joanne Lawrence and her son were leaving. The woman looked relieved as she carried her son out the door, his tiny legs wrapped around her waist and his arms firmly latched around her neck. Tess wondered if Joanne would ever let him go.

"Is everyone okay?" Tess smiled as she greeted them on the porch.

"We're fine." Joanne answered. "I'm just so glad he's safe. Thank you for everything you did tonight Tess."

"Oh, well, I think the men and the dogs deserve our thanks tonight. They all pulled together to find this handsome little guy and bring him back to you safe and sound. Everyone's just glad he is home."

Tess tapped the little boy on the shoulder, "How're you doing Gavin? Feeling okay?"

"Yep," the boy chirped. "Mommy said I can have some hot chocolate when we get back to our cabin. And Derby can have a marshmallow!" Tess laughed as she touched the little boy's cheek.

"Then you better get back to your cabin right away." She squeezed Joanne's arm as the woman gave Gavin another big hug.

Tess knelt down beside Derby and gave him a rub under his chin. The big dog licked her cheek and pushed his broad muzzle into her chest, knocking Tess off balance. "Good job out there tonight Derby. We all know you protected Gavin. He's lucky to have such a great friend."

Tess stood and watched as the three of them walked down the

cobblestone path. She felt thankful for the love of a mother, the naïve spirit of a child and the loyalty of a dog.

"It's like they're a brand-new family," Max whispered as he walked out on the porch and stood behind Tess. "How's Toto?"

"He's not good." Tess said as she sat her exhausted body down on the faded green Adirondack chair. "Brandon looked really concerned when I left." Tess paused and looked up at Max, "I hope he is okay tomorrow."

"I'm sure he'll be fine. You should get some rest now Tess. You look exhausted." Max stood next to her and wrapped his arm around the wooden post as Blue nudged his body against Max's legs. "This stray dog was pretty amazing out there," Max said as he stroked the dog's head. "He guided all of us right to that little boy. It was like he knew exactly where he was. It's a good thing he was here."

Max paused but Tess could tell he had something more to say.

Max continued. "Maybe this dog was meant to be…. well, you know, meant to be here…. with you." He stumbled over his words, obviously embarrassed by what he and Tom used to call Oprah moments.

Tess quickly answered to save her friend from blushing. "Yes, he's a pretty amazing dog. I kind of hope nobody claims him so he can stay here, but I guess we'll have to wait and see." Tess lifted herself from the chair. "I'm going to go have a hot shower and call it a night. You're going to stay, right?" Tess didn't want Max making the drive back to Kilter Falls at this hour.

"I'll just crash in the guest room and head out first thing in the morning.... right after you make me a delicious home cooked breakfast," Max joked as he wrapped his arm around Tess's shoulder. She nudged him in the ribs with her elbow and smiled.

Tess shuffled her way into the kitchen as the early morning sun bounced off the walls and filled the room with a soft hazy glow. Normally, she would be heading down to the beach for her morning swim but today she just wanted to enjoy a cup of coffee out on the porch and watch the sunrise. She stared out the window onto the property below. The sandy beach was rippled from the wind and water and the loons were singing their familiar song. The Lodge was so beautiful at sunrise.

Then Tess noticed a figure sitting at the end of the dock, wrapped in a blanket of morning fog. It was Brandon, his dog by his side, both looking out onto the lake. Tess stood motionless by the window, watching, hoping for a sign that the old Shepherd felt better today. But there was no movement except for Brandon's hand, gently moving over the dog's body. Tess poured her cup of coffee and stepped out onto the dew dampened porch. As she leaned her body against the waist high railing, she heard the click clack of Blue's paws on the floor inside.

"Well…. look who decided to wake up," Tess called as she turned and stepped back into the kitchen. "I guess you're probably looking for your breakfast, aren't you?" She bent over the dog and scratched him behind his ears, letting him lick her face to say good morning.

Tess gathered some fresh ingredients from the refrigerator and began making Blue a delicious breakfast. "Let's hope today is a little less eventful than yesterday, eh Blue? I think it would be nice if this was just an ordinary day here at Beckett Lodge." Blue barked and Tess knew he agreed. "Okay boy, here you go. Now remember, don't gobble." But the dog devoured the food in a few mouthfuls like he had the day before and then sat patiently and pathetically waiting for more. "That's all you get buddy," Tess laughed as she picked up Blue's bowl from the floor.

Tess placed the dog bowl in the sink and peeked out the window again, looking to see if Brandon and Toto were still perched at the end of the dock. The two were still there. Brandon was still looking out onto the lake, as Toto lay beside him, resting his head on his owner's lap.

Tess looked down into Blue's deep brown eyes, "Maybe we should go make sure they're okay."

Tess stepped off the porch onto the cool grass in front of the Lodge, her eyes focused on Brandon's back. The image of a man sitting at the end of the dock with the tranquil sounds of morning echoing in the distance, reminded her of the day Tom died. Tess felt the bumps rise on her forearms and a chill shake her body as memories of that day flashed through her mind. She had been standing at the kitchen window watching Tom cast his line into the lake, secretly hoping he would finally catch the "big one", when Tom suddenly dropped his fishing rod and folded over at the waist. Tess watched as he rolled forward off the dock and into the water, unconscious. She swore her feet never touched the ground that morning, when she raced to the water's edge to save her husband. But despite everything she did to revive him, he was already gone. So, she held him in her arms, on their beach, on a morning just like this.

As Tess's bare feet slide off the last granite step, Blue suddenly stopped and sat down. Tess paused and looked down at the Retriever. She wasn't sure why he had decided not to continue, but figured it may be best if Toto was still not well. She softly tip toed toward the dock.

Tess stepped quietly onto the dock but the loose boards creaked under the pressure and alerted Brandon Bishop of her arrival. He glanced over his shoulder toward her but turned back to the water without a greeting.

"Hi Brandon," she whispered, stopping a few feet behind him.

He looked over his shoulder toward her again. His eyes remained lowered and he answered softly, "Hi Tess."

"I don't mean to interrupt but I wanted to make sure you were both okay. How's Toto feeling?"

Brandon didn't answer. Instead there was a silent pause as he continued to stare out at the lake, stroking Toto's fur. Tess's eyes fell to the big Shepherd lying on his side, feet stretched out in front of him, his head comfortably resting on Brandon's lap.

Brandon coughed as he cleared his throat to speak. His voice cracked slightly as he whispered, "He's gone. He took his last breath a few minutes ago."

Tess cupped her hand over her mouth to muffle the sound of her cry. Her eyes became blurry with tears as she sank to her knees behind Brandon. She reached out and gently squeezed his arm. "I'm so sorry Brandon." She felt a tear roll from her cheek as she lowered her head, unable to look at the lifeless dog stretched across the dock.

Brandon sniffled and continued looking out into the quiet morning fog, "I'm glad he went so peacefully, in such a beautiful spot. He's in a better place now, free from pain." He paused and cleared his throat again. Tess knew he was trying to hide his vulnerability, here in front of a woman he barely knew. "I'll be checking out today. I left my keys in the cabin."

"Of course," Tess sighed. "Is there anything else I can do?"

"No. I'm just going to sit for a few more minutes and then we'll be leaving for home."

"Take your time," Tess whispered.

Tess knew it was time to leave the two of them alone. She pushed herself to her feet and stepped back. She felt a sad connection to Brandon in that moment. They had both lost the friend who meant the most to them at the edge of this lake.

She reluctantly walked away from the man and his dog, avoiding the creaking planks, careful not to disturb the silence. Blue was still sitting on the grass with a watchful eye and he greeted her calmly as she stepped off the dock back onto the grass. Tess gave him a quick pat on the head and began to slowly climb the cold granite steps leading back to the Lodge. Tess couldn't be sure but she thought she heard Brandon's cell phone ringing in the distance.

Annoyed, Brandon struggled to get his ringing cell phone out of the pocket of his shorts. He knew it was stupid, but he didn't want to disturb Toto, whose head still lay contently across his lap. Before he even looked at the number, Brandon knew it was his boss calling. James York had been trying to reach him, but he hadn't been able to answer; not with everything that had happened last night. He tried to quickly cough away some of his grief before he answered.

"Hey Boss," Brandon said softly.

"Bishop? Where have you been? This is the third time I've called!" York's voice sounded irritated.

"Sorry about that sir. They don't have great cell service up here," Brandon lied.

"Well, I told you I would update you on any developments in the Porchman case and we've found something pretty significant. Do you remember the shed you and Toto searched the night we were looking for the girl?"

"Yeah," Brandon's ears perked up at his mention of the shed.

"I won't get into all of the details over the phone but we went back to that shed and…. let's just say, we found enough evidence in there to put our suspect away for a very long time. Turns out that old dog of yours has a pretty good sniffer after all.   Why don't you and Toto come home and help us wrap this case up."

Brandon took the phone away from his mouth and pushed it under his chin so his boss wouldn't hear the sadness in his voice. "Okay Boss," he answered. "We'll head home today."

He ended the call and began to weep. He stroked the dog's head and whispered to him, "You did it boy. They're going to put that guy away for a long time because of you. I'm so proud of you and I'm sorry I ever doubted you. I hope you can forgive me." Brandon bent over and put his face close to the dog's muzzle, no longer feeling his warm breath against his cheek. "Let's go home old friend."

Brandon wiped the tears from his eyes and gently moved the dog's head from his lap, leaving behind a warm shadow and dusting of fur on his shorts. He gathered the dog in his arms and began the lonely journey home.

As she reached the main Lodge, Tess could hear Gavin Lawrence's tiny voice, echoing amongst the whistles of birds calling through the trees. She looked toward the cabin and saw Gavin leap down the porch steps and begin running toward her. She quickly wiped her eyes, hoping he wouldn't notice that she had been crying.

"Hi Tess!" Gavin shouted.

Tess waved. The little boy looked very excited about something as he clumsily raced toward her, his tiny sandals slapping along the flagstone.

"Tess, guess what?" Gavin asked out of breath.

"Hey Gavin, what's up?" Tess wiped her cheeks once more.

"Me and Mommy are going to the store and Mommy's going to get a bathing suit so me and her can swim at the beach today!" Tess couldn't help but smile at the little boy's excitement. "And Mommy said we'll get some special treats for Derby too.... since he made me safe."

Tess knelt down and ruffled the little boy's hair as she answered, "Well, it sounds like you and your

Mom and Derby are going to have a very special day today."

"Yes. We are! Will you come swimming with us too, Tess?"

"I just might, Gavin. You better go now, looks like your Mom is ready." Tess stood and waved to Joanne who was holding Derby's leash, neither one taking their eyes off the energetic youngster.

"Okay, bye Tess!" Gavin called as he sprinted back to his Mom who was waiting for him with open arms and a smile. Tess laughed and shook her head as she watched the little boy trip over an uneven patio stone and fall into his mother's legs. Joanne hugged him and checked his knees for scrapes as Derby pranced around, licking the boy's peanut-butter smeared face.

"Morning," a voice called from the porch of the main Lodge.

"Morning, Tess replied. She hadn't even noticed Max standing there, coffee in hand, wearing Tom's pajama bottoms that she had lent him the night before. "Couldn't find a brush?" she teased looking at his tangled brown hair.

"Hey, messy hair is hip these days you know."

"Not at your age," Tess quipped.

She was trying to be jovial, but Max could see right through it. He knew her well enough to know that something was wrong. But he also knew not to pry, so instead, he just asked if she wanted a cup of coffee.

"I'd love one," she replied.

The two stepped into the Lodge kitchen and as Max handed her the coffee, he had already prepared for her, he noticed

Brandon carrying Toto up from the dock. He turned and looked at Tess. "How's the old Shepherd?"

Tess bit her lip and looked at the floor. "He died this morning."

Max didn't say another word; he quietly walked toward Tess, took the coffee from her hand and placed it on the table. He gathered her into his arms and held her close. Tess felt the warmth of his body as she buried her face in his chest. "I feel so guilty," Tess whispered, her voice muffled by Max's shirt.

"You have nothing to feel guilty about Tess," he said softly, breathing his words through her hair. "You didn't know any of this was going to happen. None of this is your fault. That dog did an amazing job out there last night and he died with honor and dignity." Max gently pulled her cheek away from his body, and lifted her chin with his hand. "Everything is going to be okay." Tess knew his words went deeper than the events of the morning; he had told her the same thing over and over again after Tom died and in time, she had come to realize he was right. Everything *was* okay. She was okay. And this pain that she was feeling would lessen in time.

Tess looked into Max's brown eyes and nodded at his reassuring words. As she held his stare, she had an odd feeling wash over her. She felt like she was seeing Max for the very first time. Even with his tangled hair and ratty t-shirt, she saw a handsome and wonderful man who cared for her with a fierce loyalty and protection that she had only felt once before, from Tom.

But before Tess could tell Max how thankful she was for him, Blue barked and nudged Tess's leg.

"I think someone is jealous," Max told her.

Max loosened his hold on Tess as she bent down to scratch the dog's ears. "Are you jealous?" she asked Blue. "I hope not, because if I have my way, the two of you are going to be part of my life for a very long time."

"Well, I know I'm not going anywhere. Not until I get that home cooked breakfast I was promised." Tess snorted at Max's comment. He always knew how to make her laugh.

"Alright, let's go make some breakfast." Tess patted her thigh and called for Blue to come. She tossed her curls over her shoulder just as the phone rang at the front desk of the Lodge.

"I'll grab that," she told Max. "You start the eggs. Over-easy for me, please." Tess walked quickly down the hall, so she wouldn't miss the call.

"Good Morning, Beckett Lodge," Tess answered as she pulled the phone to her ear.

"Yeah," a man's unfriendly voice responded bluntly. "I think you have my dog? A Retriever?"

It was the call Tess had hoped would never come. Her heart pounded hard in her chest as the man's words echoed in her ear, her thoughts suddenly jumbled. She slowly lowered the phone and quietly placed the receiver on the desk without an answer. She could still hear the voice on the other end, muffled and angry through the black plastic, asking again if the dog was there. But she couldn't answer. She couldn't even move.

Finally, Tess picked up the phone and apologized, "Sorry about that, sir. We must have had a bad connection." The man asked again whether she had found his lost dog.

Tess had every intention of telling him the truth but instead, she apologized again and lied about the dog. "I'm sorry sir. I did find a stray dog here yesterday, but he ran off and I haven't seen him since." The man grunted and hung up just as Blue and Max came walking down the hall. Tess quickly hung up the phone hoping Max hadn't overheard any of her conversation.

"Was someone looking to book a cabin?" Max asked.

Tess lied again and said, "No, wrong number," as she started back toward the kitchen.

Tess faked a smile and gave Blue a scratch behind his ear as she walked past. Suddenly, she felt nauseous about what she had just done. She was normally such an honest person, usually to a fault, but this time, something in her heart told her to lie. Blue was meant to be here. He was special and she needed him. Besides, she told herself, the man's voice on the other end of the line sounded angry and there was no way she could hand Blue over to someone like that. Maybe there was a reason the dog had escaped from him in the first place. Tess shivered with uneasiness. She could only hope that her lie wouldn't come back to haunt her someday.

Tess sat down at the dining room table as Blue curled himself around her feet. She looked down at the dog, as Max started talking about his fishing plans for the day, and prayed that today would be an ordinary and uneventful day at the Lodge.

Tess quickly glanced behind her as she ran into the blinding white snow. The man, dressed all in black, was running toward her with increasing speed, his long black coat billowing around his legs and his fur-topped boots kicking up a cloud of snow as he ran.

Tess stumbled as she tried to pick up speed, the ankle-deep snow swallowing her feet like quicksand. She could feel the icy wind of winter's first storm relentlessly whipping at her bare cheeks, but oddly she couldn't hear it whistling in her ears. All she could hear was the pounding of her own breath and the snapping of ice under foot.

The ice on the lake was only a few inches thick this early in the winter, and Tess knew running on it was dangerous, but she had no choice. She had to keep running.

Tess could barely see Blue up ahead of her. The Retriever's silky blonde fur was almost completely camouflaged by the blowing snow. She prayed that Blue, the stray dog who had come into her life and completely stole her heart a few months ago, could lead her to safety and protect her from the faceless stranger who was chasing her across the lake she loved.

Panicked, Tess turned her head once more to see if the man was any closer. He was gone. But Tess kept running, not trusting that the man had simply disappeared into the blizzard. She looked again, turning all the way around, slowing her pace to a backward walk to look for the man amidst the snowy shadows. She held her hands at the side of her face to block the snow from stinging her eyes as she scanned the lake for any sign of the man.

Tess' heart pounded hard against her chest as she stood alone, exposed to the harsh winter weather and the unknowing danger that lurked beyond the wall of white. As she struggled to catch her breath, Tess spun in circles, trying to make out any sort of landmark from the shoreline; something that would help her get back to the Lodge. But it was no use. She was completely surrounded by wind-whipped snow with nothing to follow but her instincts.

Tess cinched the hood of her parka firmly around her face and started running again, hoping she was heading back toward the Lodge. The ice cracked and shifted under her feet as she ran, sending a haunting rumble out toward the centre of the lake. Suddenly, a new feeling of terror washed over her. She had completely lost sight of Blue.

She tried to call for him but the cold wind stole the breath from her lungs and made her chest burn. Tess tried again, knowing that Blue would not be able to hear her over the howl of blowing snow, and if he did, he would never be able to find his way back to her in near-zero visibility. She called for him over and over, each time stopping and listening for his familiar bark. But the only thing she could hear was the wind.

  As she stood, Tess quickly realized that her adrenaline was wearing off and the bitter cold was taking its toll on her body. She was starting to feel tired and weak. Tess hunched over, her hands on her knees, trying to muster up enough energy to get off the lake before hypothermia set in and claimed another winter victim of the Northern wilderness.

Clumsily, she started walking. Her boots felt heavy, like concrete weights around her ankles. Tess prayed that the skies would open up and the snow would stop just long enough for her to see the shoreline. She kept her head down to shield her face from the wind, lifting it only to call for Blue.

Then, Tess heard a sound in the distance. She stopped and listened, holding her breath, straining to hear the sound over the wind.

Then she heard it again.

She was certain it was Blue, barking loud enough for her to hear. Tess started running toward his cry. Her legs were tired and heavy and the snow seemed deeper than before, but she knew she had to get to Blue.

Tess trudged through the snow, calling for her beloved dog. She knew he was close by, she could feel it, but she couldn't see him. She kept calling his name, running to him, until Blue's bark was close and constant.

Then, as if her prayers had been answered, the wind calmed and the squall stopped just long enough for her to see Blue, standing in the snow with windswept fur and his nose to the air. Oddly though, he wasn't moving toward her, even though she was screaming his name.

Tess thought maybe he had been injured during the chase and was unable to move. She tumbled toward the motionless dog as the wind and snow strengthened around her again, pushing her to her knees. With no energy left to stand, Tess crawled toward Blue, struggling through the now knee-deep snow. As she got closer, Tess spotted the faint outline of a red object lying in the snow beside Blue. She squinted as she studied it, quickly recognizing it as Blue's red woven leash; the one Max had embroidered with Blue's name and given her as a gift last month. The blood red color was a stark contrast against the pristine porcelain snow.

As she crawled closer to Blue, she could see one end of the leash was attached to the dog's collar, held tight by a single silver clasp, but the other end was eerily hidden beyond the whiteout of snow surrounding Blue. Tess slowly pulled down the hood of her jacket to get a better look. She wanted to move closer to the dog, to comfort him and make sure he was okay, but she was paralysed by fear.

Then, almost as if she'd
expected it, the leash began to lift
from the top of the icy snow and
the man draped all in black,
stepped out holding the other end
of Blue's leash. Tess inhaled so
hard she felt her lungs fill the
entire cavity of her chest.

"Tess," the man's deep voice
growled as he stepped toward her.

Tess tried to scamper away on
her hands and knees through the
deep snow as the man lunged

forward and grabbed her by the shoulder.

"Tess," the man yelled.

Tess felt the man's hand tighten on her shoulder as she struggled to get away. To be Continued....

Book #2

(Beckett Lodge Series)

True Blue

**Now Available in Large Print

Only on Amazon**

Printed in Great Britain
by Amazon

23161885R00136